She is . . .

WONDER WOMAN

★ THE AMAZING AMAZON ★

CHAPTER 1

GIGANTA'S REVENGE

Reporters and TV crews crowded the front steps of the grand Gateway City Museum of Antiquities. The tall, well-dressed director himself stood on the top step, smoothing his hair as everyone scanned the skies.

"She said she'd be here," a camera operator muttered.

A reporter smiled over at him. "She still has a couple of minutes. She'll be here. Wonder Woman keeps her promises."

Moments later, the reporter pointed towards the sky. "See? There she is now!"

Wonder Woman dropped past Gateway City's skyscrapers to land on the steps, next to the director. She held a magnificent shield.

"Is that it?" a reporter shouted. "The famous Golden Shield of Dolos?"

"It is," Wonder Woman said. She held up the shield so the news photographers could get good shots of it.

"It is said that this shield – a gift to the Amazons from the god Dolos – will repel any attack its holder faces," Wonder Woman continued. "But it is more valuable as a work of art than as a weapon. And so my mother, Hippolyta, Queen of the Amazons of Themyscira, has agreed to lend it to this museum for a week-long exhibit celebrating world peace."

The director stepped forward, smiling proudly. "In three days, Wonder Woman will formally present the shield to the museum," he told them. "The event will kick off the World Peace Charity Gala."

* * *

Giganta hurled her last dart at Gorilla Grodd's picture. The dart slammed into the wall, right between his eyes.

"Bullseye!" the villain muttered. Just one more hole in a picture covered with them. It didn't help her get revenge on her former partner who had once landed her in prison. But it made her feel a tiny bit better.

The TV droned on in the background of her small hideout. Something about some boring museum exhibit. She sighed and began to pull darts from the wall.

Sticking darts in Grodd's picture wasn't nearly as satisfying as she'd hoped it would be. What she really wanted to do was punch a hole in the gorilla mastermind himself. But so far, she hadn't worked out how to do it.

Then the words "Golden Shield of Dolos" caught Giganta's attention. She turned to see Wonder Woman holding up a golden shield on TV. The mythical weapon was supposed to keep the one who held it safe.

"Grodd always wanted that shield," Giganta muttered. She knew he didn't believe in its magic. He thought the shield's metal gave it its power. "If it even works at all. After all, Dolos is a god of treachery."

Giganta shrugged. She didn't care if it worked or why. She only knew that Grodd would try to steal it. And so she wanted to steal it, too, from right under his nose.

"I'm going to take his prize and show Grodd I'm not just another pretty face," she muttered. "He should never have abandoned me to rot in prison when he could have rescued me so easily!"

Giganta turned back to the picture and threw her handful of darts, one by one.

THOK! THOK! THOK! THOK! THOK!

They landed right between Grodd's eyes.

"Playtime's over," Giganta said. "It's time to learn everything I can about that museum. It's time to make a plan!"

* * *

Three days later, Wonder Woman flew towards the museum carrying Dolos' shield. No one at the gala tonight would have any idea how difficult it had been to talk her mother into lending out the artefact.

"It isn't a weapon," Wonder Woman had argued. "Its purpose is to repel attacks, not cause them. It's a work of art that belongs in an exhibit dedicated to peace."

Queen Hippolyta hadn't looked convinced. "A villain can find an evil use for anything," she had said darkly. Then she had sighed. "Take it. But don't let it fall into evil hands. And bring it back to Themyscira in one piece."

"I will," Wonder Woman had said.

* * *

On the night of the big gala, Giganta wore her most elegant dress. It was short and extremely stretchy. She hoped it was stretchy enough to adapt to her power to increase her size. She would have to mingle with the other guests, and she didn't want to draw anyone's attention by wearing shredded clothes.

Before leaving her hideout, Giganta took one last look in her mirror. She was very tall and beautiful. She fluffed her red hair and smiled. She was going to outwit Grodd and look her best while doing it.

When she arrived at the museum, Giganta avoided the front of the building, with its towering pillars, banks of stairs and reporters snapping pictures. She tiptoed around to the side of the building where a wall of windows faced the museum grounds.

Peeking inside, she saw a high gallery crowded with stylish men and jewelled women. Waiters carrying dainty snacks and trendy drinks moved among the partygoers. Everyone was talking and laughing. They marvelled at the spectacular artefacts sitting on pedestals and hanging on walls. A string quartet played in the background.

Then the museum director cleared his throat and everyone fell silent. He made a short speech. Then Wonder Woman stepped forward and handed him the Golden Shield of Dolos. He thanked her and placed it on a specially prepared pedestal. Then everyone clapped enthusiastically.

"Wonder Woman! She could be a problem," Giganta muttered. For a moment she was worried. Then she shrugged. "No way! I've thought of a way to handle her. I've thought of everything!"

Giganta backed silently away from the windows and checked her watch. So far, everything was going according to plan.

The villain crept to the rear of the building and squinted up at the roof. Even in the dark, she could see the railing that edged the roof three storeys above.

"Perfect," Giganta muttered. She knew from her research that the railing surrounded a rooftop sculpture garden. That garden would make getting into the building easier.

Hidden in the shadows, Giganta grew larger and larger until she could easily reach the railing. She grabbed hold of it and, still holding on, shrank to her normal size. Then she pulled herself over the railing and landed lightly on the roof.

Giganta looked around cautiously. She saw statues, plants and a snack bar, but no people. No one was here. She hadn't set off any alarms. Yet.

The villain smiled.

From her research, Giganta knew there were two ways into the museum from the roof – the lift and a maintenance staircase that led down to the ground floor.

Giganta walked to the lift. Museum officials might have left it working so gala attendees could visit the roof. But when she pushed the button, nothing happened.

"Good," Giganta said. "That means I'll set off the roof alarm for certain."

Giganta tried the handle of the rooftop maintenance shed. It was locked. She grinned and pulled on it hard.

BANG! The door flew open.

BRANGA·BRANGA·BRANGA! The alarm sounded. Now her timing had to be perfect.

Giganta darted through the doorway. Beyond was an open maintenance staircase. She leaped over the railing and grew larger as she dropped through the centre of the stairwell. When her feet touched the ground floor, the villain shrank to her normal size.

Clattering footsteps were coming Giganta's way. She slipped into a supply cupboard, leaving the door slightly ajar so she could peer through the crack.

Wonder Woman flew past her – literally! Responding to the alarm on the roof, the hero soared up the middle of the staircase. The museum guards stomped up the steps behind her.

Excellent! Giganta thought. She had set off the alarm on purpose to draw Wonder Woman and the guards away from the gallery. *I can't believe how well it worked!*

Giganta watched as Wonder Woman and the guards left through the shed door. Now, once again, she'd have to act fast.

The villain checked her dress. It wasn't torn or stretched out. She could easily pass for one of the museum guests.

Giganta smiled as she stepped out of the cupboard and slipped into the public area of the museum. She hurried towards the main hall, following the sounds of music and conversation. The alarms were still clanging, but the closer she got to the gallery, the fainter the noise seemed.

Between the conversation and the music, it's amazing that even Wonder Woman heard the alarm, Giganta thought. She grinned. *In seconds the Golden Shield of Dolos will be mine!*

Giganta had almost reached the gallery when the music and conversation suddenly stopped. She shrugged. She supposed that the director was going to make another boring speech. One she would soon interrupt!

If the next few minutes go as smoothly as the last, Giganta thought, *this caper is going to be a piece of cake!*

The villain chuckled to herself as she stepped into the room. Then she stopped and stared. The people weren't just silent and attentive. They were frozen in place.

Gorilla Grodd, wearing a jetpack, was hovering in the air high above the crowd. The villain held everyone in the gallery – partygoers, waiters and musicians alike – under his telepathic mind control.

While the people stood, unable to move and helpless to stop him, the genius ape mastermind swooped down. He reached for the magnificent Golden Shield of Dolos.

CHAPTER 2

GIGANTA'S GLORIOUS GETAWAY

Grodd's back was to Giganta. He hadn't seen her, not yet. But she knew his power. Grodd had used mind control on her once, and she had hated it. She would have to act fast – while he was distracted – or she wouldn't be able to act at all.

Giganta grew almost instantly to twice, three times, four times her normal size. As the gorilla's fingers brushed the shield, her giant hand shot out and knocked him aside.

As Grodd tumbled backwards in the air, he saw Giganta grab the golden shield in her massive fist. The gorilla quickly spun in mid-air to face her. He still controlled the crowd with his mind.

Should I send the gala attendees to attack Giganta? he thought. *No, that won't help me win the shield. I'll focus my power on the giantess herself!*

Grodd concentrated, sending Giganta the telepathic command: *You are frozen in place. You cannot move. You cannot speak. You cannot think. You must drop the shield.*

The telepathic waves sped towards Giganta.

Oh no! I didn't hit him hard enough, Giganta thought in a panic. *He's seen me now! I'm doomed!*

Giganta instinctively raised her hand, trying to protect herself from the mental attack she knew was coming. And that hand held the Golden Shield of Dolos.

The telepathic waves struck the shield and bounced right back at Grodd himself. The gorilla stopped suddenly, hovering frozen in mid-air. He was unable to move or think.

Giganta could hardly believe her luck. *The shield actually works!* she thought gleefully. *And now that Grodd's learned just how useful it is, he's going to lose it! To me – his own despised ex-partner!*

Giganta was almost giddy with delight.

Then she realized that Grodd had lost control of the gala attendees when the telepathic wave had struck him. Freed from his power, the people would soon wake up. A few were beginning to blink already.

Giganta didn't know how long the telepathic blast would keep Grodd frozen. *Some of those people have phones,* she thought. *They'll call the police. Even worse, Wonder Woman will return. I have to get out of here!*

Giganta slammed her giant fist hard against the museum's wall of windows.

CRASH! The windows shattered. *KRAKK! SMASH!* Plaster cracked and wood splintered.

BAR·HOOM! The stone facing on the outside of the museum toppled. Massive stones smashed to the ground.

Giganta dashed through the huge hole and into the night air.

KLANGA·KLANGA·KLANGA! More alarms sounded. The roof creaked as the ceiling began to sag.

Giganta didn't even look back. She just ran with the shield clutched in her hand.

* * *

Wonder Woman was doing a final check of the roof when – **CRASH!** – she heard breaking glass. The building shook. Then more crashes. More alarms.

What is going on? Wonder Woman asked herself. She leaped into the air and dived over the side of the building. Then she hovered above the rubble.

The outside wall of the gallery has been destroyed, the hero realized. *It just collapsed. But what caused it? Was the museum attacked?*

Wonder Woman whirled around. For an instant a giant figure – a woman holding a golden disc – was lit by the city lights. Then she disappeared behind a skyscraper.

"Giganta!" Wonder Woman muttered. She had faced the villain before.

"What is she doing–?" And then she realized – Giganta had stolen Dolos' shield!

Wonder Woman started soaring after the villain when the building behind her gave a loud **CREAK!**

The hero whirled, looking back at the museum. *That destroyed wall was helping to hold up the museum!* she realized.

Now, with the wall gone, cracks ran up the side of the building. The floors above it sagged. Unless Wonder Woman acted fast, the museum would collapse. People would die. Valuable artefacts would be lost forever.

The Amazon warrior spun around and flew straight into the hole. She soared over the heads of silent, stunned-looking people.

Wonder Woman braced her hands against the sagging ceiling and shoved with all her might. She was strong – as strong as Superman. She would have to hold up the ceiling until everyone had escaped, and the museum's treasures were safe.

In her rush to support the crumbling building, Wonder Woman hadn't yet noticed Gorilla Grodd. He still silently hovered halfway down the gallery.

* * *

Grodd was slowly recovering from his reflected telepathic attack. He still couldn't move. But at least now he could think.

Grodd remembered Dolos' shield. How Giganta had reached for it. How he had tried to control her mind. And then he remembered nothing else.

The gorilla blinked blearily. The shield was gone. One of the gallery walls had disappeared. It didn't take a genius to work out what had happened. Giganta had stolen the shield. And now that Grodd knew how well its magic worked, he wanted it more than ever!

Slowly Grodd began to move. A finger. A toe. His head.

A loud **CREAK** alerted him to trouble. Grodd looked up and saw Wonder Woman hovering near the ceiling. He waited for her to attack. Nothing happened.

Then Grodd chuckled.

She's holding up the ceiling! he realized. *She can't let go or the building will collapse on the people waking up from my mind control! I can simply fly out of here, and she can't stop me!*

Grodd saw Wonder Woman looking at him. He saw the surprise on her face as she discovered he was there, and her dismay as she realized she was helpless to stop him.

VROOOM! Grodd revved his jetpack. Then, giving her a sarcastic salute, he flew past her. He sailed above the heads of the dazed crowd and out of the massive hole in the museum.

* * *

Wonder Woman watched Grodd disappear into the night.

Gorilla Grodd is in on this too? she thought. *He's flying after Giganta, but he looks angry. Are they still partners? Or has she stolen something that he wants?*

Wonder Woman knew saving the people below was the right decision. She knew protecting the gallery's art was important.

But I talked my mother, Queen Hippolyta, into lending the museum that shield, she thought angrily. *In a way, I'm responsible for this disaster. And I'm stuck here, when what I really want to do is pound Grodd and Giganta into dust!*

* * *

Grodd flew over Gateway City's streets. He had no trouble following Giganta. Flattened cars. Crushed trees. Shrieking citizens. She had left quite a trail.

Grodd rounded a skyscraper and spotted Giganta easily. She was at the end of Main Street, heading towards the entrance to the famous Gateway Bridge.

Traffic was light at this time of night, but Grodd spotted a bus up ahead.

Excellent! the villain thought.

Grodd sent a telepathic order to the bus driver. *A giant woman is coming. Speed up and swerve your bus into her path – NOW!*

Giganta didn't notice the approaching bus. It slammed into her foot at top speed. She tripped over it, began to fall and put out her hands to catch herself.

The shield flew from her fist and rolled across the street. *KLANG!* It slammed into a kerb.

Grodd zipped past the fallen woman and snatched up the shield. Carrying his prize, he flew up the entrance to the bridge. Glancing back, he saw Giganta stumble to her feet and begin to race after him.

Good! I have big plans for you! Grodd thought as he controlled his speed. He flew just fast enough to stay out of Giganta's long reach.

"You should have simply shrunk to your normal size," Grodd called back as he got onto the bridge. "It would have been easier to hide from me that way."

"I didn't want to hide," Giganta puffed as she raced after him. "I wanted you to see – to know that I outwitted you!"

"That was your goal all along?" Grodd taunted as he soared above the traffic. "Seriously?"

"You always underestimate me," Giganta said, running after him, dodging cars, trying not to trip over lorries. She didn't notice the cars that swerved and skidded and crashed behind her.

"You left me to rot in prison when you could have freed me easily," Giganta continued. "I want you to know I am no longer your partner. I am now your enemy!"

Grodd had almost reached the central tower halfway across the bridge. He sneered back at her. "You've made that clear enough. And you must now face the consequences."

The gorilla jetted higher into the air, up over the massive cables that held up the suspension bridge. "As if a fool like you could truly challenge the genius that is Grodd!" he shouted.

Then, making a sharp turn, Grodd veered away from the bridge.

Giganta stopped and stared. Grodd was flying out over the open bay!

No, not quite open! she thought.

Fog was rolling in. But through its wisps, she could see an abandoned lighthouse standing, dark and silent, on a distant rocky island.

"You won't get away from me that easily!" Giganta shouted. She held her breath and vaulted over the bridge railing.

SPLASH!

Giganta dropped into the bay.

She sank down, down, down through the water until her feet touched the rocky bottom. Then she began to grow taller still.

As Giganta's head rose from the waves, she saw Grodd land on the upper deck of the distant lighthouse. She slogged through the bay after him.

CHAPTER 3

BEAUTY BECOMES THE BEAST

Wonder Woman hovered against the ceiling, holding up the gallery. She waited impatiently while museum workers removed the artefacts. Then a specialized construction team used giant braces to hold up the sagging ceiling.

Finally everything was in place. The foreman yelled, "We've finished, Wonder Woman. You can let go now."

Museum workers, guests, police and construction workers stood outside the museum. They watched through the hole, holding their breaths.

Carefully, Wonder Woman stopped pressing against the ceiling. She listened for the creaks and cracks that would signal the beginning of a collapse. But all was silent.

Slowly, the Amazon Princess settled to the ground. She was ready to zip up again if the ceiling started to sag. But the braces held.

Wonder Woman walked out through the giant hole onto the museum grounds where everyone waited. The museum director stepped forward.

"Thank you, Wonder Woman," he said. "If you hadn't been here, people would have been hurt. I'm just sorry the Amazons' shield was stolen."

"It wasn't your fault," Wonder Woman answered. "I blame myself. I promised my mother I'd keep it safe."

Wonder Woman leaped into the air and hovered, looking down at the crowd. "Don't worry, Director," she said. "I'll restore the treasure, and I'll get the thieves who stole it!"

Wonder Woman looked off into the distance. A swathe of bent trees, damaged buildings and partially flattened cars and lorries extended as far as the eye could see. Police cars and ambulances crowded the streets, lights flashing and alarms blaring.

Giganta certainly has left a clear trail of destruction, Wonder Woman thought. *Following her will be easy!*

Then she realized, *It must have been easy for Grodd to follow her too!*

Wonder Woman flew down Main Street, above the wreckage and flashing lights. At the entrance to the Gateway Bridge she found a bus tipped on its side. Its passengers were crowded around, talking excitedly.

Wonder Woman landed and offered to help. The emergency workers said everyone had escaped with only minor injuries.

"Do you know what happened here?" Wonder Woman asked the crowd.

"I saw a giant woman!" a little boy said.

"And the bus ran into her and tipped over," his sister said. "Then the giant fell and dropped something shiny, and this flying gorilla grabbed it!"

"And then she chased after him!" the boy said excitedly, pointing up to the bridge. "They went up there!"

"Thank you!" Wonder Woman said. It sounded like Grodd now had the shield.

Wonder Woman flew up and hovered above the bridge. Cars clogged the lanes, as usual. Traffic was at a standstill.

But instead of the usual cars crawling along, the bridge was now a jumble of wrecked cars. People crowded on the sides of the bridge against the high railing.

Wonder Woman followed the wreckage to the middle of the bridge. Beyond the central tower was a huge traffic jam. Drivers were honking their horns, but the destruction ended at the centre of the bridge.

So where have Giganta and Grodd gone? the hero thought.

Wonder Woman looked around. People were pointing towards Gateway Lighthouse.

"I saw them!" she heard a woman tell an elderly man. "A flying gorilla and a giant woman!"

"He flew that way," a teenager said, pointing. "And she jumped into the river after him!"

That answered Wonder Woman's question. She flew past the bridge railing and out over the bay, heading towards the abandoned lighthouse. Fog was rolling in. It was getting harder to see.

But as she flew closer, the details became clearer.

Lighthouse Island jutted up in the middle of the bay. The old lighthouse was topped with a watch room surrounded by a railed deck called a gallery. Above the gallery was a glass-paned lantern room. This room had its own narrow deck and railing.

That old lighthouse isn't much more than a forgotten relic of an earlier time, Wonder Woman thought. *What are Grodd and Giganta doing there?*

Wonder Woman circled wide around the lighthouse. The fog had grown even more dense. She hoped it would hide her while she found out what was going on.

As Wonder Woman drew closer, she heard a loud **SPLASH!** Giganta rose from the water – hair and clothes dripping – and began to climb up the steep, stony island.

The villain had grown huge – as tall as the lighthouse. She cupped her hands and peered into the lantern room.

"I saw you go in there, Grodd," Giganta shouted. "Give me the shield, or I'll smash you like an insect!"

FLASH! A blinding light hit Giganta full in the face. Waves of energy played around her body.

"What's happening?" she gasped.

Gorilla Grodd stepped out onto the deck surrounding the lantern room. Giganta was trapped, frozen in the blinding light.

Grodd studied her with a superior smile. "You have been caught in the beam of my DNA resequencer," he said. "Since you insist on behaving like a mindless animal, you will now become one."

"What–?" Giganta spluttered. "But–"

HA! HA! HA! Grodd laughed. "Just look at yourself!"

Giganta stared down at her body in horror. Her arms grew longer. Her legs grew shorter. Hair sprouted all over her body.

"No!" Giganta cried. She put her hands to her face. Her brow jutted forward. Her mouth became more muzzle-like.

"What have you done?" she groaned.

"You are the first in this city to become my gorilla subject, Giganta," Grodd said. "But you won't be the last!"

* * *

Hovering, half hidden by the fog, Wonder Woman watched horrified as Giganta's shape became increasingly ape-like.

The woman is a villain, Wonder Woman thought. *But she doesn't deserve that.*

The Amazon warrior knew she had to save her. Wonder Woman flew around to the back of the lantern room and peered through the glass.

Grodd had attached strange machinery to the lighthouse lantern. The beam shining from it made flickering lights play across Giganta's skin. Somehow that was causing her transformation.

Grodd watched Giganta as she morphed into a gorilla. "I'm so glad you're helping me test my equipment," he taunted. "It's so satisfying to transform you while you are aware of your own destruction."

Grodd's telepathy! Wonder Woman thought. *I'll have to move like lightning to escape it. I dare not let myself fall under his control!*

Wonder Woman flew at the lantern room feet first.

CRASH! The Amazon's boots smashed through massive panes of glass. She hurled herself into the villain's DNA resequencer and toppled it towards him.

But as the machine fell, Grodd whirled and whipped up Dolos' shield. The smashed machinery flew right back at Wonder Woman. **WHRAMMM!** It slammed into her and knocked her over, burying her beneath a pile of twisted metal.

"That was just my prototype, my test machine," Grodd said. "My real resequencer is elsewhere. In minutes, a beam hundreds of times stronger will sweep across the city. Everyone it strikes will be remade in my image. I will be their lord and master. And with this shield in my hands, no one, not even you, can stop me!"

Wonder Woman shoved off the heavy equipment and struggled to stand. She was ready to face Grodd, ready to stop him.

But when she looked around, the gorilla mastermind was gone.

CHAPTER 4

TRICKING THE TRICKSTER

Wonder Woman flew out of the smashed lighthouse window. She hovered, scanning the bay for Grodd. The fog was clearing now, but Grodd had disappeared.

"Where is he?" the hero murmured. "Can he actually change the citizens of Gateway City into apes?"

"Him can! Him change me!" The choked cry came from below. "Now me just an ugly monster!"

Wonder Woman glanced down. She'd been so focused on finding and stopping Grodd that she'd almost forgotten Giganta.

How could I forget a giant ape woman? Wonder Woman sighed. *Which proves just how dire this situation is.*

The giantess hadn't completely turned into a gorilla. Her skin sprouted hair, and her body and face looked more ape-like, but she was still a giant. And her dress, though soaked in water, still looked glamorous.

For an instant longer, Wonder Woman ignored Giganta. She squinted through breaks in the fog, studying the city.

The Amazon Princess realized there were five mountains and six skyscrapers tall enough for Grodd's second DNA resequencer. She only had minutes to stop him, and she couldn't check all of them in time.

Wonder Woman turned to Giganta. "Did you see which way Grodd went?"

Giganta sneered sulkily. "Me villain! Why me help you?"

"I smashed Grodd's DNA resequencer before you changed completely," the Amazon said. "You can still speak. You can still understand what I'm saying."

Wonder Woman held her breath awaiting Giganta's reply. All of these things were true – though Giganta clearly wasn't as clever as she had been.

Giganta looked up at Wonder Woman suspiciously. "Me know where Grodd go," she said. "Maybe me tell if me can come with you."

"Come with me?" Wonder Woman asked. "Why?"

"Me help capture Grodd! Me get revenge on him!" the giantess roared. Then the mutated villain collapsed onto the rocky island in a depressed heap.

"Me want big, beautiful self back," Giganta said in a small, sad voice.

"All right, you can come," Wonder Woman said. "If we reach the remaining resequencer in time, I think I know a way to change you back. But we have to hurry."

Giganta leaped to her feet and pointed towards a skyscraper on the far shore. It towered above the other buildings. "There!" she said. "Grodd go that way!"

The hero flew towards the skyscraper. The ape woman waded into the bay and surged through the water after her. When Wonder Woman arrived at the building, she hovered out of sight and studied it carefully.

The skyscraper rose in levels, like a tall, narrow wedding cake. Stone gargoyles decorated the corners of each level and a glass-walled observation deck ringed the very top. It offered sweeping views of the city.

"That's the perfect location," the Amazon murmured. "A beam shining from the top of that building will cover much of the city and strike a lot of people."

Wonder Woman rose cautiously, keeping another building between her and the tower. She wanted to stay out of sight, but she also needed to see what Grodd was doing.

And there he is, Wonder Woman thought, spotting Grodd through the glass wall of the observation room. The room was crowded with massive machinery. It looked larger and more dangerous than the resequencer in the lighthouse.

Large enough to transform a city! Wonder Woman thought.

Grodd moved around the machine feverishly, setting dials and moving levers. A large switch – like a massive lever – poked out from the front of the device.

That must be the switch that turns on the resequencer, Wonder Woman thought. *Now where's Dolos' shield?*

There! Wonder Woman spotted it, lying on a table where Grodd could grab it at the first sign of trouble.

Wonder Woman heard a splash far below and looked down. Giganta was climbing out of the bay.

The Amazon warrior flew down and hovered beside the ape woman. Giganta looked up at the tall building sadly.

"Grodd did not used to have powers," Giganta said. "But him made mind control helmet. And then somehow helmet gave powers to him brain. He more fun when him just ordinary mad genius gorilla mastermind."

Wonder Woman nodded. "I understand," she said. "Maybe we can fix that too. Now here's the plan."

* * *

Wonder Woman stood on the shore, looking up with a little smile as Giganta began climbing up the skyscraper. *Like King Kong,* she thought. *If Kong were a giant ape woman in a glittery dress.*

Stop staring and start moving! Wonder Woman told herself sternly. *This city isn't going to save itself!*

Keeping out of sight behind a nearby building, the Amazon warrior rose into the air. She peeked around the corner. She needed to know what Grodd was doing now!

Grodd had turned away from the windows. Wonder Woman could see his back as he hunched over a dial on the resequencer.

Grodd was definitely moving more slowly now. More surely. It looked like he had almost finished fine-tuning his equipment.

Meanwhile, Giganta reached the building's final level and began her climb towards the observation deck.

"Hurry, Giganta!" Wonder Woman murmured. "I don't think there's much time left!"

Ten storeys. Nine storeys. Eight . . .

I have to move now! the Amazon thought. *This plan needs split-second timing to have any chance of working.*

Wonder Woman raced towards the glass-walled room. Grodd reached for the massive lever. Giganta pulled herself over the railing of the observation deck.

KRASSHH! The giant smashed her massive fist through the glass wall.

Grodd whirled around. His mouth gaped wide with surprise, but he was ready to repel any danger. He snatched up the shield and held it out. At the same time, Grodd reached out for Giganta's mind with his vast telepathic power.

SMASH! The Amazon warrior crashed through the window behind him at top speed. **WHAM!** She slammed into his back, knocking him off balance.

Wonder Woman flipped up and over Grodd, snatched the shield from his hand, and hovered between him and Giganta. Grodd's mind control ray struck the shield and bounced back at him.

"Not again," the gorilla groaned. Then the ray struck him, freezing him in place.

Giganta grabbed Grodd in her giant hand. "Now me crush to bits!" she growled.

Wonder Woman leaped into the air. "No," she shouted. "You can't crush him!"

"Me can!" the ape woman said. "You watch me!" She squeezed her fist tighter.

"Only Grodd knows how to work this machine," the Amazon said. "If you want to change back, you'll have to let him go!"

Giganta frowned. "How we know he can fix me? Grodd bad guy. Can't be trusted."

Wonder Woman held up her Lasso of Truth. "Do you know what this is?" she asked.

The ape woman frowned. "It magic rope. Make people tied up tell truth."

The hero smiled. "That's right. I'll make him tell us how to fix you – and he'll have to tell the truth. That's how the magic works."

Wonder Woman glanced over at Giganta. "You don't have to stay large, you know. You can shrink down to normal size now."

As Giganta shrank down, Wonder Woman tied her golden lasso around the frozen Grodd. Then she held up Dolos' shield while she and Giganta waited for him to wake up.

It took a few moments, but finally Grodd blinked. Slowly, he began to move. And finally, he was himself again.

Grodd struggled angrily, but Wonder Woman had tied the knots tight. He couldn't get away.

The villain glared at the women. Wonder Woman could tell what he was thinking.

"Don't," the hero said. "I have the shield now. Any attempt at mind control will crash back on you, remember? Do you really want to knock yourself out again?"

"You want something," Grodd growled. "What is it?"

"You change me back," Giganta said. "I not want to be monkey woman!"

"Ape!" Grodd corrected her. "Gorillas are apes. Apes don't have tails."

"Whatever," Wonder Woman said, rolling her eyes. "I want you to tell me how to turn her back."

Grodd sneered. "Why should I?"

Wonder Woman smiled. "Because you have no choice. The lasso that binds you compels truthful answers. My first question is: Can the equipment in this room change Giganta back into a human?"

Grodd tried not to answer. Then he tried to lie. When that didn't work, he blurted out the truth.

"Yes," he grumbled. "If the settings are correct."

"YES!" Giganta leaped into the air.

"Good!" said Wonder Woman. "Now let's get started."

CHAPTER 5

THE FINAL DOUBLE-CROSS

Wonder Woman carefully followed Grodd's grumpy instructions. She reset every dial. She adjusted every control. And finally the resequencer was ready.

Wonder Woman pointed to a spot right in front of the massive machine. "Stand there," she told Giganta. "And I'll pull the lever."

The ape woman stomped over to the spot, glaring at Grodd.

"Don't worry. I don't think it will hurt," Wonder Woman said. "You'll probably just feel a light prickling along your skin."

"Do it," the ape woman said.

Wonder Woman placed her hand on the lever. "Okay," she said. "Three . . . two . . . one . . . Now!"

Wonder Woman forced down the lever.

With a bright flash of light, energy played all around Giganta. She began to change shape. Her legs got longer. Her arms got shorter. Her fur disappeared. Her face lost its ape-like look.

Wonder Woman switched off the machine. Giganta turned and looked at her reflection in the window glass.

"I'm me again!" Giganta cried. "I can talk and think! And Grodd is our prisoner—"

Giganta glared at Grodd. "But we can't leave him like that. The second the shield is gone – or the lasso is removed – he'll use his mind control to escape."

"And then threaten the world again!" Wonder Woman said. She turned to Grodd to ask him a few more questions.

"Can your DNA machine wipe the telepathic powers from your mind?" Wonder Woman asked.

Again Grodd tried not to answer, but the lasso's magic made him talk.

"Yes!" he roared angrily.

"Can it restore your brain to the way it was before your mind control helmet gave you telepathic powers long ago?"

"Yes!" This time Grodd said it sulkily. He knew what was coming.

Wonder Woman asked a third question: "How do I set up the DNA resequencer to do that?"

And Grodd had to tell her.

* * *

Grodd glared at the Amazon Princess as she followed his instructions. She turned each dial and moved each lever carefully.

"That shield should have protected me!" he muttered. "Why did it work sometimes and not others? Why were you able to attack and defeat me?"

Wonder Woman adjusted the final dial. "The shield works as Dolos intended," she replied. "He promised that it would repel any attack its holder faces. But Dolos is a trickster god. And when you get gifts from tricksters, it's wise to look for tricks."

Wonder Woman aimed the energy projector at Grodd. "Dolos said the shield will repel any attack its holder faces, remember? It says nothing about protecting against attacks from behind."

GRWARRR! "I should have known!" Grodd howled his fury.

"You have not defeated me! Not forever!" Grodd roared. "I'll just create another mind control helmet and get my powers back!"

Wonder Woman shrugged. "Then you'll have to do it from prison!" she said.

She turned on the machine. The bright ray of light struck Grodd full in the face. Crackling energy surrounded him.

Wonder Woman glanced over at Giganta. "Grodd's mind control abilities are gone," she said. "No more–"

Then Giganta frowned. She was slowly backing towards the hole in the observation deck's glass wall – and she was holding Dolos' golden shield.

"Sorry," Giganta said. She stepped through the hole onto the outer deck and began to grow huge.

"Well, I'm not really sorry," Giganta said. "Dolos' shield is just too useful for a super-villain to pass up, especially now that I know how the trick works. It was fun teaming up with you. Really. Except for the ape part. But our partnership is now over."

Then Giganta started climbing down the outside of the building.

HA! HA! Grodd laughed. "I'm not the only one who was tricked," he said. "Maybe that giantess is smarter than I thought!"

Wonder Woman was angry with herself. *I let my guard down,* she thought. *After working together, I tricked myself into thinking Giganta was on my side.*

Wonder Woman had to go after Giganta. She had to get back Dolos' shield. But she also had to keep Grodd from escaping. She would have to leave him tied up with her lasso until the police arrived.

The Amazon warrior dashed through the shattered glass wall and leaped into the night sky. She hovered, searching the outside of the building for Giganta.

The villain was climbing down faster than she had climbed up. She was almost halfway to the ground now. But she still had almost fifty storeys to go.

If I can sneak up on her, I might be able to capture her quickly, the Amazon thought.

ZOOM!

Wonder Woman shot through the air like a bullet, planning to tackle Giganta off the wall. She had nearly reached the giantess when the villain heard her coming and held out the shield.

WHAMPHH!

Instead of slamming into Giganta, the shield hurled Wonder Woman backwards.

The Amazon Princess righted herself in mid-air. While she recovered, Giganta climbed down another ten storeys.

Wonder Woman sighed.

This is going to be a lot harder than I'd first thought, she realized. *Maybe I can distract Giganta without actually attacking her. Perhaps I can make her lose her grip on the building and make her fall.*

Wonder Woman flew towards Giganta again, but this time she didn't attack her. She zipped up and down. She buzzed around the giant's head, dropped towards her huge feet, and then darted up again.

Giganta kept letting go of the building to swing the shield at the Amazon, trying to use it to swat her like a fly.

Wonder Woman saw that Giganta had almost reached the bottom level. She was about to place her massive foot on the gargoyle that jutted from the corner.

And suddenly the Amazon Princess knew exactly what she had to do.

Wonder Woman flew at the giant villain, circling her head rapidly. Giganta swatted at her with the shield, waving it around wildly. The villain made sure the shield faced the Amazon at all times.

Giganta now clung to a narrow windowsill by the fingertips of one hand. One of her giant feet gripped a lower windowsill with its toes. The other foot felt for the stone gargoyle just below her.

Wonder Woman, who had been darting around Giganta's head, suddenly dropped like a stone. As she fell she smashed the lower windowsill.

WHAKKK! Giganta lost her footing.

CRAKKK-CRASH! The Amazon warrior smashed into the gargoyle. The stone statue broke away from the building and hurtled towards the deserted street below.

Giganta was dangling from the windowsill by the fingertips of one hand. But it wasn't made to hold the massive weight of a giant.

CRACK! The windowsill gave way.

Giganta screamed as she fell towards the ground far below. She dropped Dolos' shield and flung out both hands. She tried to grab hold of the building once again – to catch herself. But it was too late. She was hurtling towards the pavement below.

Wonder Woman flew under Giganta and caught her before she could hit the ground.

KRASH! KRASH! The buildings shook as the rubble smashed into the street below.

KLANGGGG! The metal shield slammed onto the pavement.

As Wonder Woman dropped with Giganta, she pulled a rope from a flagpole. *I'll need something to tie Giganta up,* she thought. *Once she's small enough, that is.*

Wonder Woman grunted a bit and wavered, pretending to have trouble.

"Shrink back to human size," the hero called to Giganta. "You're so large and heavy, I'm afraid I'll drop you."

"O-okay!" Giganta stammered. "G-good idea!" She began to shrink. And slowly, Wonder Woman sank towards the pavement.

The Amazon Princess quickly bound Giganta's hands while the villain was normal size. "Stay that way!" she told the villain. "If you grow large now, the rope will cut through your hands."

Wonder Woman could hear sirens approaching. *Someone called the police,* she thought. *Not surprising, considering all the noise we made.*

All in all, the police of Gateway City were having quite an interesting night.

* * *

Wonder Woman turned Giganta over
to the police. They cuffed her with power
dampers so she couldn't change size to
escape. Then they put her in a police van.

Meanwhile, the Amazon warrior carried
down Gorilla Grodd. The police put power
dampers on him as well. Wonder Woman
told them his mind control powers had been
removed, but they still didn't trust him. She
didn't trust him either.

As they put Grodd in the van, Giganta
smiled at Wonder Woman.

"No hard feelings, okay?" the villain said.
"I appreciated your help – putting me back
to normal and, especially, putting Grodd in
prison. But you know–" Giganta shrugged,
"I really had to try and take that shield. I
am a super-villain. And that sort of thing is
practically in the super-villain handbook."

Wonder Woman sighed as she watched the van drive off. Then she bent down to pick up the smashed disc. It was all that was left of the once beautiful Golden Shield of Dolos.

* * *

The Amazon Princess flew back to the museum. She landed next to the director, who was still watching as the construction workers continued to brace the building.

Looking up at the ruins of the gallery, the director thanked her for her help.

"But perhaps you should just take the shield back to Themyscira," the director said. "Maybe we shouldn't display any more magical artefacts. They're just too tempting for super-villains."

"My mother would agree with you," Wonder Woman said.

The hero showed him the smashed shield and told him what had happened.

"The shield tends to make the one who wields it careless," Wonder Woman said. "That's why we Amazons never used it. And why we were willing to lend it out as art."

Slowly, Wonder Woman flew into the air. "I'll take what's left of it back to Themyscira and tell my mother what happened. I'm sure she'll say, 'I told you so!'"

Wonder Woman glanced sadly at the flattened disc. "I did promise to return it in one piece. And, in a way, at least that's one promise I'm keeping."

GIGANTA

BASE:
Metropolis

SPECIES:
Mutated Gorilla

OCCUPATION:
Criminal

HEIGHT:
1.97 metres or taller

WEIGHT:
Varies

EYES:
Blue

HAIR:
Red

POWERS/ABILITIES:
Size-shifting, super-strength and invulnerability. As a giant she is almost as strong as Wonder Woman.

BIOGRAPHY:

Giganta's history with Grodd runs deep. The gorilla mastermind actually created Giganta by changing an ape into a human woman. In the process, he gave her the power to increase her size to towering heights – and her strength along with it. For a time, Giganta partnered with Grodd. She was even the most loyal member of his Secret Society, until a run-in with the Justice League landed her in prison. By the time Giganta got out, another super-villain had taken her place beside Grodd, and Giganta's feelings towards him soured. Now the size-changing super-villain typically works alone, and her criminal capers often put her in the cross hairs of Wonder Woman.

· The Secret Society isn't the only villainous organization Giganta has joined. She once served as a member of the Legion of Doom. In an interesting twist of fate, she even helped the Legion defend Earth against an invasion by the super-villain Darkseid.

· Giganta is one of Wonder Woman's most destructive enemies. Her enormous size and super-strength make it almost impossible for her not to crush cars, damage buildings and topple bridges while committing crimes. Wherever she goes, Giganta leaves a path of destruction in her wake.

· Although Giganta is difficult to stop, Wonder Woman's superpowers often give her the edge in battle. The Amazon Princess relies on her super-strength when going toe to toe with the powerful giantess. And her ability to fly is particularly handy whenever Giganta grows to new heights.

ABOUT THE AUTHOR AND ILLUSTRATOR

Louise Simonson enjoys writing about monsters, science fiction, fantasy characters and super heroes. She has written the award-winning Power Pack series, several best-selling X-Men titles, the Web of Spider-Man series for Marvel Comics and the Superman: Man of Steel series for DC Comics. She has also written many books for children. Louise is married to comic artist and writer Walter Simonson and lives in New York, USA.

Luciano Vecchio was born in 1982 and is based in Buenos Aires, Argentina. As a freelance artist for many projects at Marvel and DC Comics, his work has been seen in print and online around the world. He has illustrated many DC Super Heroes books, and some of his recent comic work includes *Beware the Batman*, *Green Lantern: The Animated Series*, *Young Justice*, *Ultimate Spider-Man* and his creator owned web-comic, *Sereno*.

GLOSSARY

artefact object made by human beings, especially a tool or weapon used in the past

compel make someone do something

consequence result of a person's actions

DNA material in the body's cells that gives people their individual characteristics

gargoyle grotesque human or animal face carved from stone that projects from the side of a building

genius unusually intelligent or talented person

mythical imaginary or possibly not real

resequencer machine that changes the order of something

sarcastic use of mocking words or gestures meant to make fun of someone or something

telepathic relating to communication from one mind to another without speech or signs

transform make a great change in something

treachery betrayal of trust

DISCUSSION QUESTIONS

1. Giganta steals the Golden Shield of Dolos as a way to get revenge on Gorilla Grodd. Which does she want more, the shield or revenge? Why do you think so?

2. When the museum's ceiling is about to collapse, Wonder Woman decides to hold up the roof. What were the consequences of this decision? Could she have handled the situation any differently?

3. Gorilla Grodd wants to change everyone in Gateway City into apes. If you had a machine that could transform people, what would you change them into and why?

WRITING PROMPTS

1. The Golden Shield of Dolos protects the person who wields it from any danger he or she faces. Imagine you had a magical item. What would it do? Write a short description of your magical item and draw a picture of it.

2. Giganta has the power to change her size. Imagine you had the same power. Where would you go and what would you do? Write a short story about your adventures.

3. At the end of the story, Wonder Woman plans to return the damaged shield to her mother, Queen Hippolyta. Write a short scene, using dialogue, about what happens when she takes the artefact to her mother.

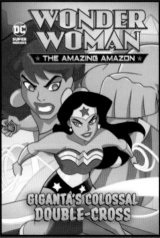

JACK LUDLOW is the pen-name of writer David Donachie, who was born in Edinburgh in 1944. He has always had an abiding interest in history: from the Roman Republic to medieval warfare as well as the naval history of the eighteenth and nineteenth centuries, which he has drawn on for his many historical adventure novels. David lives in Deal with his partner, the novelist Sarah Grazebrook.